Eeny, Meeny, Miney Mole

J A N E   Y O L E N

illustrated by Kathryn Brown

Voyager Books
Harcourt Brace & Company
San Diego   New York   London

First Voyager Books edition 1996

Library of Congress Cataloging-in-Publication Data
Yolen, Jane.
Eeny, Meeny, Miney Mole/written by Jane Yolen;
illustrated by Kathryn Brown.—1st ed.
p.   cm.
Summary: Three moles live underground, and then one of them finally
ventures upward to find out what the world is like "Up Above."
ISBN 0-15-225350-5
ISBN 0-15-201007-6 (pbk.)
[1. Moles (Animals)—Fiction.]   I. Brown, Kathryn, 1955–   ill.
II. Title.
PZ7.Y78Ee   1992
[E]—dc20   91-6466

C D E F G

A B C D E (pbk.)

Printed in Singapore

The paintings in this book were done in Winsor and Newton
watercolors on Winsor and Newton watercolor paper.
The display and text type were set in Kennerly
by Harcourt Brace & Company Photocomposition Center,
San Diego, California.
Color separations were made by Bright Arts, Ltd., Singapore.
Printed and bound by Tien Wah Press, Singapore
This book was printed with soya-based inks on Leykam recycled paper,
which contains more than 20 percent postconsumer waste and has a total
recycled content of at least 50 percent.
Production supervision by Warren Wallerstein and Diana Ford
Designed by Camilla Filancia

For Frankie after her first Spring . . .
— J. Y.

. . . with love
— K. B.

There were once three sisters who lived at the bottom of a deep,
dark hole. Their names were Eeny, Meeny, and Miney Mole.
In that hole, dark was light, day was night, and summer
and winter seemed the same.

Sometimes the sisters went to bed at dusk and rose at dawn. Sometimes they went to bed at dawn and rose at dusk. And sometimes they never

went to bed at all. That will happen when dark is light and day is night and summer and winter seem the same.

One time when Eeny was out burrowing on the left side of the hole, she met a worm who told her the most astonishing thing.

She hurried back to the hole, leaving a trail of dirt behind.

"I have just heard the most astonishing thing," she announced to her sisters. "I have heard that Up Above"— which is what they called the world on top of the ground— "things are both dark *and* light."

"Nonsense!" said Meeny.

"Silliness!" said Miney.

"Don't trust passing worms," they said together.

Then they went to bed and pulled the covers up over their heads because they didn't want to even *think* about light.

But Eeny could not sleep. She wandered around the hole thinking about light. She wondered if it was big or little; if it was round or long. She wondered if light spread from corner to corner Up Above like a blanket or if it just touched in and out like the thread in the hem of a dress. She thought all these new and complicated thoughts for hour after hour. She was still thinking when her sisters got up.

Another time when Eeny went out burrowing on the right side of the hole, she met a centipede who told her the most astonishing thing.

She hurried back to the hole, leaving a trail of root snips behind.

"I have just heard the most astonishing thing," she announced to her sisters. "I have heard that Up Above there is both day *and* night."

"Nonsense!" said Meeny.

"Silliness!" said Miney.

"Don't listen to addlepated centipedes," they said together.

Then they went to the kitchen and dipped their noses into their soup bowls and snuffled up tubers so they didn't have to think about day.

But Eeny could not eat. She wandered around the hole thinking about day. She wondered if day was short or tall; if it was quiet or loud. She wondered if day was sharp like hunger or soft like sleep. She thought all these new and complicated thoughts for hour after hour. She was still thinking long after her sisters were full.

The next time Eeny went out burrowing on the underside of the
hole, she met a snake who told her the most astonishing thing.
She hurried back to the hole, leaving a trail of bark behind.

"I have just heard the most astonishing thing," she announced to her sisters. "I have heard that Up Above there is both summer *and* winter."

"Nonsense!" said Meeny.

"Silliness!" said Miney.

"Never ever even *speak* to snakes," they said together.

Then they went into the living room and began to play checkers, Meeny with the red pieces and Miney with the black, so they didn't have to think about summer and winter.

But Eeny could not play. She wandered around the hole thinking about summer and winter. She wondered if they were low or high; if they were young or old. She wondered if they were damp and clumpy like the dirt on the underside of the hole or dry and crumbly like the dirt near the top. She thought all these new and complicated thoughts for hour after hour. She was still thinking when Miney won the third game.

The very next time Eeny went out, she didn't burrow to the right or to the left of the hole; she didn't burrow under or behind. She burrowed up and up, thinking astonishing and frightening thoughts, until she broke through the crumbly top and right into Up Above.

She stuck her nose into Up Above.

She stuck her head into Up Above.

She heaved her whole body into Up Above and walked around.

Light *did* spread from corner to corner like a blanket above her. But it also touched in and out of tall trees like a thread.

Day *was* sharp, but the shadows were soft, and she liked the way they curved around into night.

There was a strange moistness to the air, a little like tears, that was sometimes warm and sometimes cold. She could not tell if it was winter or summer or something in between. But there was a murmur all around, of bees and trees, of showers and flowers, of tadpoles and tidepools and crinkly grass.

The murmur turned into a name. Spring!

Eeny smiled.

Then she went back to her hole, digging down and down, leaving a trail of dirt and grass snips and bits of fresh bark behind.

"Day is nice," she said out loud. "And light. I am glad to have visited both. They are new and complicated. And someday I will meet summer and winter as well." She sighed and kept digging down and down, a bright yellow flower as sweet as a murmur clutched in one paw.

"But just wait till I tell my sisters about Spring!"